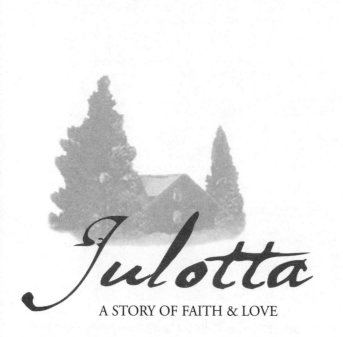

Julotta

A STORY OF FAITH & LOVE

©2002 by Tracie Peterson

ISBN 1-58660-584-4

Layout design by Anita Cook.

All Scripture quotations are taken from the King James Version of the Bible.

Julotta is a reprint of "God Jul," originally published in *An Old Fashioned Christmas,* Barbour Publishing.

Published by Promise Press, an imprint of Barbour Publishing, Inc., P.O. Box 719, Uhrichsville, Ohio 44683, www.promisepress.com

 Member of the
Evangelical Christian
Publishers Association

Printed in the United States of America.
5 4 3 2 1

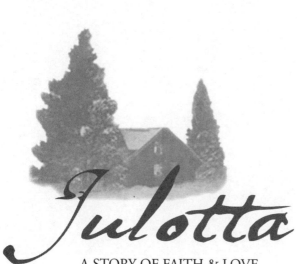

Julotta

A STORY OF FAITH & LOVE

TRACIE PETERSON

PROMISE PRESS
An Imprint of Barbour Publishing

OSTKAKA
(Swedish Pudding)

2 EGGS	2 QUARTS MILK
1 CUP CREAM	½ RENNET TABLET
½ CUP FLOUR	½ CUP SUGAR
¼ TSP. SALT	

Oven at 400°F

Beat eggs and ½ cup cream together, add flour, and mix until smooth. Add salt. Heat milk to lukewarm and add mixture. Soften rennet tablet in a spoonful of water and add to mixture, stirring slowly until evenly mixed. Let stand for 10 minutes then bake in hot oven at 400°F for 30 minutes. Then turn oven down to 350°F and bake for 1 hour. Take out of oven and pour remaining ½ cup of cream and sugar over it and bake at 350°F for an additional 20 minutes. As the pudding is formed, the whey (milky liquid) may threaten to run over, so use a deep pan. Serve with sweetened berries.

o n e

$\mathcal{S}$igrid Larsson stared in stony silence at the pine casket. Inside, her mother's body lay in final rest, and even now as the pastor spoke of the resurrection to come; Sigrid felt a terrible loss. She had built her life around her mother's needs and now she was gone; and at twenty-seven, Sigrid felt she was far too old to start a new life.

Even if I wanted to start over, she chided herself, *what would I do? Who would have me, an old spinster with nothing to offer?*

She looked around the circle of mourners to find friends and family whom she cherished dearly. She was alone. They had each other. They were husbands and wives and children, and together they made up families. Her family had started out to include a mother, father, sister, and brother, but now they were gone. Father had died fifteen years ago in a railroad accident, and with that one stroke of fate, her life had changed. At twelve she had been forced into adulthood in many ways.

"Let us close by singing together," the pastor stated, then boomed out the words of a well-known hymn in a deep heavy bass.

Sigrid mouthed the words, uncertain that she could actually sing. How could one sing when their heart was so heavy? She glanced up to find Erik Lindquist staring at her with a sympathetic, yet otherwise unreadable expression. His blue eyes were the same shade as her own, a rather pale, icy blue. His blond hair, straight as string as her mother would have said, was parted down the middle and slicked back on either side. He looked most uncomfortable in his "Sunday-go-to-meeting" clothes, and Sigrid would have laughed had the circumstance not weighed so heavy on her heart.

Erik had been her mother's hired man for the last twelve years. He owned the property next to theirs, and when he learned of the Larsson women's struggles to survive and keep the farmstead running, he had gone to Bothilda Larsson, or Tilly, as most folks called her, and struck a deal. He would farm their land, as well as his own, and split the profits down the middle. Bothilda and Sigrid would care for the dairy cows, pigs, and chickens as was in keeping with Swedish traditions. American men might take the reins of caring for the animals, but Tilly thought it funny to see a Swedish man trying to milk a cow.

The arrangement worked well for everyone, including Sigrid's brother, Sven, who had a new family and land of his own to worry about. He seemed more than happy to turn over the responsibilities of his parents' homestead to Erik. Sigrid had been the one to protest, but she knew it was of little use to argue. She couldn't very well farm the land herself, yet she had resented the interference of an outsider. Even if that outsider was a rather nice-looking, young Swedish man.

The singing had concluded and people were coming up to offer her their condolences.

"Tilly will be missed for sure," Mr. Anderson told her.

"Ja, t'ings won't be the same without her," another man assured Sigrid.

Mrs. Swanson and Mrs. Moberg both took hold of her hands at the same time and tearfully lamented the loss of their dear friend. Sigrid tried not to notice that her mother's casket was slowly being lowered into the ground.

"Come along," yet another of her mother's friends announced, "we've laid food at your house, Sigrid."

Sigrid nodded and allowed the women to herd her along to the awaiting carriage. She thought it funny that she should ride when so often she had walked the distance from church to home. But the women insisted she ride, in spite of her own longing to be left alone. *Grief and mourning make folks do strange things to offer comfort,* she thought.

The Larsson farmstead was situated on the east side of Lindsborg, just far enough away to make a walk into town a good stretch of the limbs. Her father had managed to secure a prime tract of land when they'd first come to the area in 1869, and in her entire life, Sigrid had never ventured any farther than a ten-mile radius from the tiny town.

She loved her home, and her heart swelled with pride as they approached the narrow drive that marked the property. Sigrid stared at the white clapboard house and felt a real sense of peace. Her mother might be gone from her in a physical sense, but she would live on in this house and in the things that surrounded Sigrid. She would simply remain here the rest of her days, living as best she could, and always she would remember the good times she'd known when her family had all been together.

The carriage came to a halt, and before she actually realized what was happening, Erik Lindquist had appeared to help her down. She felt small beside his six-foot-two frame. He towered over her by nearly a foot, and his big, callused hands betrayed signs of hard work. Farming in Kansas was at worst a practice in futility and at best a labor of love. Her mother used to say that Job's patience had never been tested to the extent of trying to grow crops in Kansas. Sigrid smiled at the thought, and Erik seemed taken aback.

"Someone tell a joke?" he asked, leaning down to whisper in her ear.

She startled at the warmth of his breath on her neck. "No, I was just remembering something Moder used to say."

"If you were remembering Tilly's words, then I'm sure I understand."

He offered her a gentle smile and stepped away just as Sven approached.

"Sigrid, Ina and I want to talk to you."

Sigrid sighed and nodded. She could well imagine that neither her brother nor sister wanted to worry about her grieving on her own. They were no doubt going to suggest she come spend a few months living with one or the other of them. And, frankly, most folks would expect her to do something just like that. But Sigrid didn't want to leave the house. She wanted to stay on and think about her life. She wanted to watch another spring blend into summer and then autumn.

She followed her stocky, blond brother into the house and was surprised to find Ina standing alone while her husband, Clarence, herded their five children outside.

The sisters embraced and nodded at each other with stoic expressions securely fixed in place. Their family had never been given to public spectacles of grief, and as was true of many of their Swedish friends and extended family, they weren't ones for showing much emotion.

"So, what is it you wanted to talk about?" Sigrid asked, looking from Ina to Sven and back again. In the background, the clatter of dishes and women's chatter caused Sven to motion the sisters to one of the side bedrooms off of the main living area.

"Ina and I have discussed it, and we both agree

that the house should be sold immediately," Sven said, as though the matter was settled. "I've talked to Olga, and she said it would be a great help to have you around the place."

"You want to sell Fader and Moder's house?" she asked in disbelief.

It was as if no one had heard her, however, as her sister picked up the matter. "I'm happy for you to come and stay with us part of the time, as well. You could sleep with Bridgett in the loft bedroom. You know how she adores you."

Sigrid stared at them both as though the meaning of their words had eluded her. "I don't know what to think."

"That's why I figured on taking care of the matter for you," Sven said, with the authoritative air of an older brother. "I'll put up a notice and—"

"No!" Sigrid said, suddenly finding her voice. "I don't want to sell."

Ina looked at her with wide blue eyes. "What do you mean? Surely you don't want to stay on here alone. Moder wouldn't want you to be here alone."

"Of course, she can't stay here," Sven said, quite seriously.

"I'm a grown woman, Sven. There is no reason why I can't stay here. I'm fully capable of doing what work needs to be done. Erik is taking care of the farming, and the rest of the work was pretty much my responsibility anyway." She paused to settle her nerves. With only the tiniest hint of emotion in her voice, she continued. "Erik already has the ground turned and the planting will be finished within the week. I've got peas and potatoes planted, and you can't expect me to just up and let someone else reap the benefits of my labors."

"I've got plenty of peas and potatoes at my place," Sven countered. "Be reasonable, Sigrid. Ina and Clarence need the money and so do I. Last year's crops weren't that good and—"

"I don't want to move. This is my home. I stayed behind while you both married and went your ways," Sigrid protested in uncharacteristic anger. "I think I deserve to live out my days here."

"You could marry," Ina suggested. "You aren't so

very old that a bachelor or widower wouldn't see the use in having you around."

Sigrid felt as though her sister had somehow just insulted her. It wasn't that she didn't know the odds were against her finding a love match and marrying. It wasn't even that her sister spoke aloud the sentiments that Sigrid had already considered many times. It was. . .well. . .it was just more than she wanted to have to deal with at that precise moment.

"We can talk about this tomorrow," Sven said, opening the bedroom door. He looked out into the living room as if seeking someone. "Olga's going to wonder what's keeping me."

"Come stay with us tonight," Ina said softly as she turned to follow Sven.

"No," Sigrid stated firmly. "I'm not going anywhere."

Ina shrugged, while Sven rolled his eyes and grunted something unintelligible before leaving the room. Sigrid closed the door behind her sister and leaned back against it to calm herself. *How dare they try to force me from the only home I've ever known!* She felt somehow betrayed, and the only thing she wanted to do was hide away in this room until everyone else went home.

She glanced around and sighed. *Am I being foolish? Is it completely unreasonable to want to stay here, even if it means staying alone?*

A light rap sounded on the door. Sigrid bolstered her courage and turned to open it. Ella Swanson, Sigrid's lifelong friend, stood holding a bowl of ostkaka and lingonberries.

"I thought your favorite dessert might help," Ella offered.

Sigrid smiled and nodded. "You always know just how to cheer me up." The ostkaka looked most appealing, and Sigrid realized she was quite hungry. "Thank you, Ella."

"Ja, sure. You'd do the same for me."

Sigrid's smile faded. "This day has been so hard."

Ella's countenance mirrored the way Sigrid felt inside—a blend of confusion and sorrow. "Ja," Ella whispered. "Your moder was a good woman. I miss her, too."

Sigrid thought how strange she should have to struggle with such a riot of emotions in one single day. The sorrow over losing her mother was enough to keep her drawn within herself, but her anger at Sven's insensitivity to her needs threatened to burst forth without warning.

"Everything okay?" a masculine voice questioned from behind Ella. It was Erik.

Sigrid shook her head. "No. I don't think anything will ever be okay again."

"What's the matter?" he asked. Ella seemed eager to know the problem as well, but just then her mother called her away, leaving Sigrid to awkwardly face Erik alone.

"Sven wants to put the property up for sale right away," she finally managed to say. She refused to say anything else as she was desperately close to tears. Cradling the bowl in her hands, Sigrid tried to focus on the pudding and berries instead.

"I hope you won't sell it off without giving me first chance to buy it," Erik said.

Sigrid's head snapped up, and she knew without

needing to see for herself that her face clearly registered her anger. "Erik Lindquist, I have no thought to see this place sold to anyone. This is my home. I have nothing else now, and I'm tired of people trying to separate me from the only thing left me."

Erik seemed notably surprised by her outburst. Unable to bear up under his scrutiny, Sigrid pushed him aside and made her way into the living room. *I'm not going to deal with this today,* she thought, lifting a spoonful of ostkaka to her lips. The dessert seemed flavorless to her, and what would normally have been a rare treat was now souring on her stomach. Would this day never end?

SKORPOR
(Swedish Rusks)

1 CUP SUGAR	½ TSP. SODA
½ CUP SHORTENING	½ TSP. SALT
1 EGG	1 TSP. BAKING POWDER
1 CUP SOUR CREAM	1 CUP NUTS
3–4 CUPS FLOUR	

(ENOUGH TO MAKE DOUGH STIFF)
Oven at 325°F

Mix all ingredients together and pour onto a long sheet pan. Bake 1 hour at 325°F. Take out of oven and turn oven to 200°F. Then cut skorpor into strips about 1" x 4" while still in the pan and put back in the oven to dry until hard and light brown (about 1 hour). These make great dunkers for coffee.

two

$\mathcal{S}$igrid's week went from bad to unbearable. She remained firm as Sven continued to nag about selling the property, but when a town meeting was called to discuss the railroad moving into the area, she had second thoughts about maintaining her life in the quiet town of Lindsborg. Building the railroad had brought her parents from Illinois to Kansas in the first place, but the railroad had also cost her father his life.

"The railroad is bringing new life to your community," an older man in a black suit assured the crowd. "The railroad will bring new people to settle the area, and with them will come new industry and growth. A community like Lindsborg needs the railroad and," he paused to play up to the crowd, "the railroad needs Lindsborg."

The townsfolk murmured amongst themselves while Sigrid found an inconspicuous place for herself at the back of the meeting hall.

"Excuse me," a soft masculine voice whispered over her shoulder. "You aren't leaving, are you?"

Sigrid turned to find a handsome, dark-haired stranger eyeing her with consuming interest. "I'm not very interested in the topic," she managed to reply.

"Oh, but you should be." The man's brown eyes seemed to twinkle, and a broad grin was revealed beneath his thick, handlebar mustache. "I'm Ruben Carter. I work with this railroad." He said the words as though she should be impressed with such an announcement.

Instead, Sigrid dismissed herself and went outside

to wait for Sven and Erik. Both were enthusiastic, or so it seemed, to at least hear what the railroad was offering the community.

"Wait, Miss. . . ," Mr. Carter called, following her.

"I'm sorry, Mr. Carter," Sigrid said, rather stiffly. "The rail holds nothing but bad memories for me. My father was killed in a railroading accident near Salina."

"I'm sorry to hear that, Miss. . ." Again he paused, waiting for her name.

"Larsson," she replied flatly.

He gave her a sweeping bow and pulled up with a grin. "Miss Larsson, it is a pleasure to make your acquaintance."

Sigrid smiled in spite of herself. "Thank you, Mr. Carter. Now, if you'll excuse me—"

"But we've only just met," he interjected. "You can't go now. Why don't you tell me what happened to your father?"

Sigrid smoothed the dusty folds of her dove gray skirt. "He was pinned between two cars. He died soon after they were able to free him."

"I'm sorry. But you know, that doesn't make the railroad evil."

"No, I suppose it doesn't," Sigrid admitted. "But it does make me wary of having it in my town."

"Where do you live? Perhaps the railroad will be far removed from your daily routine."

Sigrid shook her head. "No such luck. We've already received a notice saying that the railroad will pass over a corner of our property. No one asked me if I wanted it there. We were simply told that it will be placed there, and we will be given a modest amount of money to compensate the taking of that which never belonged to the railroad in the first place." Her words were delivered in a stern, unemotional manner.

Mr. Carter nodded sympathetically. "I can understand, but you mustn't fret so over it."

"I believe we've adequately discussed this issue," Sigrid said and turned to go. She was barely halfway down the street when Mr. Carter caught up with her.

"At least allow me to make a suggestion," he

offered. "We will be looking for ways to feed our workers. Perhaps you would care to assist us by cooking for the railroad?"

Sigrid shook her head and continued walking. She had absolutely no desire to be responsible for aiding the railroad's entry into Lindsborg. She might not be able to stop its arrival, but she certainly didn't have to assist it.

"Wait, Miss Larsson," Mr. Carter called out again, then joined her, matching her stride.

Sigrid said nothing for several moments. She wondered who this man really was and what his part was with the railroad. Perhaps he had a great deal of money tied up in the development of Lindsborg, and maybe all of that hinged on the successful presentation of the railroad to the citizens of the small town. But most folks were quite excited about the railroad, so surely talking her into a favorable response wasn't all that important.

"Please just hear me out. If nothing else, do it for the sake of Christian charity," Mr. Carter said with a pleading expression.

Sigrid felt helpless to argue with the man. Moder had always said that God expected folks to treat one another as they would if Jesus Himself were standing in their place. "All right," she replied, looking Ruben Carter full in the face. "I'm listening."

Ruben smiled. "Would it be possible for you to have me to coffee?"

"Swedes are famous for always having a pot on the stove," Sigrid said, warming to his smile. He seemed like such a gentle-natured man, and his soft-spoken words were methodically relaxing her prejudices. "I suppose the men will be along directly," she said, glancing back at the main street of town.

"Yes, they were very near to concluding their discussion," Ruben agreed.

"All right, Mr. Carter, I will give you coffee and hear you out," Sigrid said.

"So you see," Ruben told her as she poured steaming black coffee into his cup, "the railroad likes to work with the folks of the community. We have a great many workers who set the rails in place and bring in supplies. We rely upon good folks like you to help us with the feeding and sometimes the housing of our workers." He took a drink of the coffee and nodded approvingly. "This is very good."

Sigrid smiled and brought a plateful of skorpor to the table. "These are for dunking in the coffee." She paused as his gaze seemed to roam the full length of her body before resting on her face.

"I think I've died and gone to heaven," he said, taking one of the skorpor.

Sigrid, not used to open flirting, felt her face grow flushed. As she turned quickly away, she saw out the open kitchen window that Erik and Sven were coming up the lane. Their heated discussion seemed to indicate a problem, and Sigrid could only wonder if they were discussing the sale of her home.

"So now that I know exactly where you're situated," Ruben began again, "and I know you can cook, what say you to the possibility of hiring on to fix my men breakfast each day? You'd be well paid."

Sigrid immediately thought of her brother's need for money. *What if I were to find enough or make enough money to buy out Sven's and Ina's shares of the property? Would that satisfy them?*

"How much would I be paid?"

"Oh, it depends," Ruben said, looking up to the ceiling as though to mentally calculate the matter. "If you were to provide a full breakfast—and remember those are hardworking men with hearty appetites—it could be a very satisfactory sum."

"I assure you, Mr. Carter, farmers are hardworking men with hearty appetites as well. I've fed plenty of farmhands and I know how men can eat. What I don't know is what the railroad considers satisfactory."

"Enough to cover your expenses and then some," Ruben replied. "Look, if you'll consider this, I promise to make it well worth your time and trouble. The men need to be fed before first light every morning so that they can be to work by sunup. There will probably be about twenty or so in number, and you only have to worry about the morning meal. I'll arrange other plans for the noon and supper meals."

Sigrid finally felt intrigued by the idea. She could easily feed twenty men, and making money from the railroad seemed a promising way to keep Sven from forcing her to sell the homestead. "How long will you need to keep this arrangement?" she asked, glancing back out the window to find Sven and Erik stopped at the gatepost. They appeared to be in no hurry to come inside.

"Probably six or seven months, maybe less," Ruben replied.

Sigrid turned back to find him dunking yet another skorpor into his coffee. "All right," she said, taking the chair opposite him at the table. "I will consider doing this thing, but only if you put all the details in writing. I don't want the railroad cheating me for my efforts."

"You certainly have a low opinion of us, don't you," he more stated than questioned.

"You would, too, if you'd lost your father and

found your family forgotten and destitute by the very organization that took his life." She knew her words sounded pain filled, yet Sigrid couldn't stop herself from continuing. "Frankly, I'm grateful that my mother won't have to see the railroad come to this town. It would break her heart and make it seem like losing my fader all over again."

"I'm truly sorry for your loss, Miss Larsson. My own parents are still alive, so I cannot possibly know your pain. Please believe me when I say the railroad will be honor bound in their arrangements with you. You need not fear that you will be cheated in any way."

For a moment, Sigrid lost herself in his compassionate expression. His brown eyes seemed to reach inside her with a comforting assurance that every word he spoke was true. She wanted to do nothing more than listen to his promises and know that she wouldn't have to leave her home, but the slamming of the back porch screen door brought her out of her reverie.

Sigrid jumped to her feet to get two more coffee

mugs. With emotions fading and senses returning, she called over her shoulder, "I'll do the job, but I still want it in writing."

RAGMUNKAR
(Swedish Potato Pancakes)

3 CUPS GRATED
   RAW POTATOES
½ CUP MILK
1 EGG
  (SLIGHTLY BEATEN)

2 T. FLOUR
1 ½ TSP. SALT
1 T. ONION
  (FINELY CHOPPED)

Beat egg into the milk and immediately add potatoes. Sprinkle in flour, mixing well, and add salt and onion. Fry in greased skillet, as you would regular pancakes, until golden brown.

three

Sigrid went to work immediately to prepare her house for the railroad workers. She cleared the living room of its normal furniture, with the exception of the piano and wood stove, and brought in tables and chairs from every other corner of the house. Ella had even managed to loan her an extra table, and with that, Sigrid was able to put five men to a table with enough space to accommodate them all comfortably.

31

She rose every morning at three-thirty in order to have the stove hot and the food ready for the workers. It caused some havoc with her normal routine, but after a week or two, Sigrid had worked through all the minor problems. Her supplies had used a fair sum of her funds, but she was already turning a profit. Not to mention that her jelly jar was now rapidly being filled with money. Not only was the railroad paying her to feed the men, but some of the men paid extra for things like cookies, pies, and biscuits. Sigrid was finally seeing a way to satisfy Sven, although he'd been none too impressed with her method of earning the money.

Erik was even less impressed.

As a hired hand, Erik had made a routine of sharing the morning and sometimes the evening meal with Tilly and Sigrid. He seemed to resent having to share his sanctuary with fifteen to twenty rowdies every morning. Sigrid ignored his scowls and comments that the men would just tear up the place. She was happy to have something to focus on other than her mother's death and her brother's insistence that

she move. She'd even managed to make a small peace
with the railroad. She would never embrace this mode
of transportation as being of particular importance in
her life, but she could overlook their intrusion so long
as it meant she could keep her parents' home intact.

"My, my, but aren't you the sun in the sky,"
Ruben said, as he joined the men who were filing
into the living room for breakfast.

Sigrid said nothing but glanced down at the yel-
low calico gown. It was worn, yet serviceable, and
she'd put it on with the intention of brightening her
own day. She was tired of the dark woolens she'd
worn all winter and tired of feeling a sense of loss for
her mother every time she reached for something
black. Spring was a time of colors, and Sigrid wanted
to bring such color back into her life.

"Smells mighty good in here, Ma'am," a burly
man with a matted black beard announced. "Hope
you're servin' them thar Swedish pancakes again."

Sigrid smiled. "There are whole plates of them
already on the tables, and I'll be in directly with
ham and eggs."

Ruben followed her into the kitchen and reached out to touch her arm. "I meant what I said. You are about as pretty as a picture today. I like what you've done with your hair, too."

Sigrid reached a hand up to the carefully pinned blond bun. She usually just braided her hair and pinned it up at the nape of her neck, but today she'd felt like something different. With a surprising flair of artistry, Sigrid had woven her hair atop her head, leaving wisps to fall around her face. In a moment of pure vanity, she'd even taken a fork and heated the tongs to carefully curl each wisp until it conformed to her desired style.

"It really makes you look much prettier," Ruben said. "Not that you weren't already quite pretty to start with."

Sigrid felt her cheeks grow flushed and turned in a panic to check on the biscuits. Bent over the open oven door, she hoped that the redness of her cheeks would be explained away by the heat.

"You shouldn't find my praise so embarrassing," Ruben whispered as she straightened up. "I'm quite sure any of these men would agree with me."

"You do go on, don't you?" Sigrid said, busying her hands with slicing additional pieces of ham. "You'll have to excuse me, I need to get these on the table." She lifted two large platters of ham and eggs, but Ruben took them from her and leaned close to her ear.

"Perhaps you would honor me with a walk later?"

Sigrid jumped back, startled at the way his hot breath made her skin tingle. "I. . .ah. . .I have too much work to do."

"It can wait," Ruben said with a roguish smile. "But I can't."

He left her standing there cheeks flushed and heart racing, to stare after him. Sigrid had no idea how to deal with his attention. She'd never allowed herself to enjoy the attentions of any man, and now Ruben Carter was putting her resolve to the ultimate test.

But why not enjoy it? she thought. *I'm twenty-seven years old. It's not like men are beating down the door to court me.*

Erik watched from the doorway as Carter wooed Sigrid with his smiles and words. A pang of bitter jealousy coursed through him, and he didn't like it at all. He'd known Sigrid for what seemed an eternity, but more than this, he'd loved her for nearly as long. And, he'd come to think of her as belonging to him.

He remembered the first time he'd seen her at a church youth function. At least, it was the first time he'd seen her as anything other than a child. She was fifteen, and the new pink gingham dress that she wore more than showed off her womanly charms. She had just started to pin her hair up and looked so very grown up that, for a moment, Erik had wondered who she was. It wasn't long until he realized that this was the little Larsson girl. And, she wasn't so little anymore.

As Carter passed by with the ham and eggs, he gave Erik a sideways glance. Erik, feeling rather embarrassed, realized that he was scowling. He was even more embarrassed when he found Sigrid staring at him with a questioning look.

"Something wrong, Erik?" she asked, before turning to pull biscuits from the oven.

Erik crossed the small kitchen amidst the noise of the railroad workers' hearty approvals. "This is wrong, Sigrid," he said flatly. "You have a house full of rowdy men and no chaperone to keep you from their attention should somebody get out of hand. You know what they're saying in town, don't you?"

She straightened and put the pan of biscuits on the counter. "No, I'm sure I don't. I scarcely have time to lounge around town listening to gossip."

Erik's conscience smarted, but not enough to leave the thing alone. "You're risking your reputation here, and I think that Carter fellow is way too familiar with you, if you ask me."

"Well, I didn't. Stop playing big brother to me and stay out of it."

Erik wanted to pull her into his arms and tell her that being a big brother was the farthest thing from his mind, but instead he crossed his arms against his chest. "So you don't care what people think?"

"Not when they are misjudging me without bothering to learn the truth," she said rather defiantly.

Erik wondered if he was included in that group.

Had he misjudged the situation? Was it mere jealousy that fanned his concern? He waited while Sigrid took out biscuits and coffee and tried to think of what he would say next.

When she came back into the kitchen, she looked up at him for only a moment before heading to the back door.

"Where are you going?"

"I need more wood," she said, motioning to the empty bin beside the stove.

"Let me get it," he offered.

She looked at him hard for a moment, then nodded. "All right, but you must promise no more lectures."

He smiled. "I have to promise good behavior in order to haul wood?"

He watched her fight back a smile before rolling her eyes. "No, but if you want breakfast, then you must mind your manners."

He followed Sigrid outside into the darkness of the morning and noted that the faintest light was now touching the eastern horizon. They followed the well-worn path around the side of the house, and Sigrid began picking up logs.

"Here," Erik suggested holding out his muscular arms, "just load me up." Sigrid did as he told her, and they worked silently for the remaining time.

After making three more trips, the bin was full and the coffee perked cheerily atop the stove. The day was dawning, and with it, the railroad workers were taking their leave. One by one they filed out the front door, stopping only long enough to leave bits of change in the jar by the door. Carter seemed reluctant to leave, but Erik made it clear that he was staying on and in no hurry to go about the farm's daily chores. Returning Erik's look of unspoken challenge, Carter finally donned his hat and bid a busy Sigrid good day.

"I'll stop by later," Carter assured her, "with a railroad check. Maybe you won't be too busy to take that walk then?"

"Thank you, Mr. Carter, and we shall see," she called over her shoulder, her arms filled with empty plates.

When Carter had let the screen door slam behind him, Erik picked up a stack of plates and followed Sigrid into the kitchen. He wanted to question her about Carter's mention of a walk, but he knew she'd only take offense.

"You really shouldn't wear yourself out doing this," Erik began. He wanted to plead a case that would appear entirely sympathetic to her own condition. "Getting up at three-thirty and adding this to your other chores is taking on way too much."

Sigrid laughed at his concern. "Erik, I need the money, and you know as well as anyone that a little hard work never hurt a body."

She was plunging the greasy plates into soapy water, but Erik took hold of her arm anyway and pulled her with him to sit at one of the empty tables. "I want to talk to you about all of this."

She wiped soap suds onto her apron and shook her head. "There's nothing more to be said. You heard Sven. He wants this place sold, or he wants the money entitled him. I can work hard and give him the latter, but I can't lose this place. Not yet."

Her expression softened, and her gaze traveled the interior of the room. "I'm not ready to say good-bye yet. I know it might sound foolish, but that's just the way I feel."

"I'm not asking you to say good-bye nor to sell the house, unless of course you want to include me in on the deal." He held up his hand as she started to protest. "You've got to understand, in many ways, I'm just as tied to the place as you are. After all, I've been helping to farm it for almost thirteen years."

"I know all of that," she said, her voice edged with irritation. "That's why you should understand how I feel."

"But I do," he softly replied. He studied her confused expression. Her blue eyes seemed to search him for answers, and he wondered if he could go through with what he planned to do.

"Then why can't you understand my feeding the workers?" she asked flatly. "Why can't you see that by the end of autumn the railroad will be finished, and I'll have saved enough money to buy out Sven and Ina. It's the only way."

"No. It's not the. . .only way," Erik said, hesitantly.

"Then what do you suggest?"

"You could marry me. I'd be happy to pay Sven and Ina whatever they thought fair."

Sigrid's mouth dropped open. She stared at Erik with such a look of alarm that he wondered if he'd actually offended her.

"Marry you? You must want this land bad to offer me marriage." She got up from the table, and Erik could read the anger in her eyes. "You've treated me like an unwanted little sister all of my life. When you ran around with my brother, you ignored me or else teased me, unmercifully, and when it was just Moder and me, you. . .well you—" She stopped midsentence, her face reddened from the tirade, eyes blazing in accusation. "Oh, forget it!" she exclaimed in exasperation. "Why does everyone suddenly seem intent on putting me out of my home?"

She ran from the room before Erik could offer a single word of explanation. Not that he was entirely certain that he would have even tried to speak. She was angrier than he'd ever seen her, and yet he couldn't help but smile. *Little sister, indeed,* he thought. *I've seen you as something more than a little sister for a great long while.* But this thought only frustrated him more as he remembered that Ruben Carter obviously looked upon her in other than brotherly fashion.

Leaning back in exasperation, Erik ran a hand through his hair and contemplated the situation. *How can I convince her that it isn't her land I love?*

Swedish Rye Bread

1 CUP POTATO WATER (WATER FROM A BOILED POTATO)	2 CUPS RYE FLOUR
	½ CUP ALL-PURPOSE FLOUR
1 PACKAGE OF YEAST	1 T. SALT
1 POTATO (BOILED AND MASHED)	2 CUPS WATER (OR BUTTERMILK)

Mix and leave to rise until double in size.

Boil together:

½ CUP SUGAR	½ CUP MOLASSES
¼ CUP SHORTENING	¼ CUP ORANGE PEEL (FINELY GRATED)

Oven at 375°F

Cool and put into doubled bread mixture. Work this well with 5–6 cups of flour to make a dough that doesn't stick to the board. Form into 2 or 3 medium-size loaves and let rise until double. Bake at 375°F for 1 hour.

four

A week later, Sigrid found that there were still no easy answers to the questions that plagued her mind. Erik made himself her constant companion so long as the railroad men were in the house. He was also more than attentive when Ruben Carter chose to spend time with her, and Sigrid felt great frustration with his interference.

Even now, as she pounded out those frustrations on the bread dough she was working, Sigrid found

Erik staring at her from over the rim of his coffee cup. He went later and later into the fields these days, and Sigrid knew that it was because of Ruben's attentions. *He's appointed himself my guardian,* she decided, and the thought of answering to yet another "brother" left a completely sour taste in her mouth.

"Aren't you worried about rain?" she asked, patting the dough into a ball.

Erik glanced at the window, as if contemplating her question, then shook his head. "It won't rain today. Maybe tomorrow. I've got time."

"Well, if you've so much time on your hands, you could fix that section of fence my cows keep escaping through. I did my best, but it won't do much to keep them in if they get very determined to seek greener pastures."

"You want me out of here for a reason?" Erik asked, eyeing her seriously.

She looked at him for a moment, thought of an angry retort, then bit it back and turned away. She couldn't very well tell him that he made her uncomfortable. Everyone made her uncomfortable these days. She couldn't even go to church without getting an earful of how scandalously she was behaving. It didn't matter that she was working herself to death in order to save her home from being sold.

"Well? Is that the reason? Is Mr. Carter headed back to fill your head with more nonsense?"

Erik was referring to a conversation he'd come in on earlier that morning. Ruben had been telling her about his home in Kansas City. Well, home seemed a paltry description, compared to the glorious details Ruben had offered. Anyway, it wasn't any of Erik's business, she reminded herself.

"Sit here all day, if that's what you want," she snapped and glanced out the window in time to see her brother coming up the walkway. "Oh, great. Now I'll have two of you to deal with."

"What?" Erik said, getting to his feet. "Carter is back, isn't he?"

Sigrid turned angrily. "It's Sven, if you must know. Now sit down and finish your breakfast. You might as well talk with Sven, because I have nothing more to say to either of you."

She covered the rye dough with a clean towel and went into the living room to pick up the last of the dishes. Sigrid could hear Erik greet her brother with an offering of coffee. She felt herself tense, wondering why she couldn't understand Erik's protective nature. He'd never been one to watch over her like this. Then again, Moder had always been alive to keep watch over her. *But I'm twenty-seven,* she thought with a sigh of exasperation. *I don't need someone to look after me.* Then she thought of a prayer she'd been taught by her mother.

Gud som haver barnen kar, Se till mig som liten ar.

"God who holds the children dear, look after me so little here," she whispered.

Tears came to her eyes. "Oh, Moder," she whispered. "I miss you so. I do need God to look after me. I know that. But I don't need—"

"Well, Erik said you were hard at work," Sven boomed, coming into the living room. "I don't suppose you're ready to put an end to this foolishness?" He didn't bother to wait for her to answer. "I'm tired of hearing the talk about you in town."

Sigrid gave him a casual glance of indifference. "But I suppose you aren't too tired of it to repeat what you've been bothered by."

Sven's broad face tightened at the jaw, but otherwise he showed no other expression of emotion. "Those men seem to have a right good time taking their breakfast here."

"Good," Sigrid replied and went back to wiping down the table.

Erik had joined Sven by now and added his own thoughts on the matter. "I heard your name bandied about by that Carter fellow. He's taking an awful liberty, if you ask me—"

"Well, I didn't," Sigrid replied and, gathering up her things, whipped past both men before either one could respond.

Sven was first to follow, and when he caught up with her, he took her by the arm and made her sit at the table.

"You're going to talk about selling the land," he said. "I know several people interested in buying—"

"No!" Sigrid interjected. She crossed her arms

and glared at both Sven and Erik. The men took seats opposite her and waited for her to calm.

"Sigrid," her brother began.

"No, Sven. I don't want to leave. Maybe next year. But not now. I need this house. I need to feel Moder's presence. It gives my heart peace. I need to think about what I want to do. Where I want to go. Is that so hard to understand?"

"No, but as I've already said, Ina and I could use the extra money."

"I'm planning to buy you both out," Sigrid announced, surprising her brother. "That's why I took on the job of feeding the railroad workers. Ruben, that is, Mr. Carter," she added after noting the look on Erik's face, "has seen to it that I'm amply paid."

"You think you can make enough to buy us out?" Sven asked with a look of disbelief.

"How much are you expecting to make?" she asked, happy to at least have his attention turned in a direction she could deal with.

"Well, I figured there would be at least fifty dollars for each of us. Tom Anderson said the place is worth at least one hundred fifty dollars, maybe more."

"I know I'd pay that," Erik threw out casually.

"Fifty?" she asked, her voice faltering. "Each?"

"Ja, that seems more than fair."

Fifty to each, she thought. That was one hundred dollars, not counting her own share. It might as well be a million for all the good it would do. She did a quick mental calculation and realized that if the railroad stayed in the area until November, she could amass the money needed. Maybe even by then, she could sell extra vegetables from her garden, as well.

"Give me until Christmas," she finally said.

Sven rubbed his chin and exchanged a glance with Erik. "It would be mighty hard to wait."

"Well, I can give you part of your share now, and if Ina can wait, I'll have the rest by then."

"How much you talking about?" Sven questioned.

Sigrid could see that she had his interest. "Twenty dollars."

"Twenty?" He perked up at this and rubbed his chin again. "I suppose I could wait until Christmas."

"Good," Sigrid said, jumping to her feet. She

rushed to her room and took out twenty dollars from the money she'd saved back. It didn't leave her much, but in a few weeks she would make it all up. Hurrying back, she thrust the money into Sven's hands before he could change his mind. "Now, I have work to do."

Going back to the sink, she ignored the hushed talk between her brother and Erik. *Please God, let it be enough to make Sven go in peace,* she prayed. She understood her brother's need for cash, but it hurt her that he couldn't understand her reluctance to leave the home of her birth.

"Well, I'll go then. Olga will wonder why I've been so long to town."

"Don't lose your money," Sigrid called out, turning to watch him go.

When Sven had gone, she could see that Erik had more to say. Wiping her hands on her apron, Sigrid came to sit down once again and folded her arms. "All right, speak, Mr. Lindquist, and tell me what I've done to offend you now."

Erik shook his head. "You haven't offended me.

I just wish I could explain some things to you. I wish you'd let me help."

"Help do what? Buy the farm?"

"I could help you in that way. You know I wouldn't expect you to move. Letting me help you would be a whole sight easier than working yourself into an early grave."

Sigrid could see that he was genuinely concerned and that his words were given in an attitude of sincerity. She felt her resolve crumble. He had been good to her and Moder, and to turn her back on him now would be cruel.

"Erik, you are kind to offer, but I don't think I could live here with you owning the land. I could never afford to pay for my keep and it wouldn't be right to expect you to let me live here for free."

Erik smiled. "Like I said before, we could get married. I'd be happy to pay Sven and Ina their fifty dollars, and we could even live on here if you wanted to."

Sigrid was touched more deeply than she could express. That Erik would offer himself up in that manner seemed to say that her welfare was of more importance to him than his own. "That's kind, Erik," she murmured. "Kind, but not practical for you."

"I don't want you thinking that it would just be an act of kindness," Erik said, seeming to struggle for words. "I mean. . .well—"

"You don't need to explain," Sigrid interrupted. "I know how you cared about Moder and you probably feel obligated to see me cared for, for her sake. I think, too, that you understand why I want to stay on. But, I'd like to accomplish this myself. I don't want anyone marrying me out of pity, all so that I can keep a parcel of land and a rundown house."

"Sigrid—"

"No, hear me out, Erik. It's important to me that you know how much I appreciate your offer. It shows what a good friend you really are. I'm sorry I got so mad at you earlier, but you have to understand I'm a grown woman. I can't have you telling me who I can and can't talk to, and I don't want you worrying about the men coming here to eat. God watches over me, and He knows my heart in this matter."

Erik's expression seemed almost pained. Sigrid

thought it would be better to put the matter behind them. "I've got to get to work, whether you do or not," she said, trying to sound lighthearted. She got to her feet and went back to the sink. "God will work out the details."

Erik left the Larsson house feeling more frustrated than ever. God might know Sigrid's heart, but he sure couldn't figure it out. Had she fallen in love with that Carter fellow? Why couldn't she see the trouble Carter could be? She was too naive, too sheltered. He wanted to explain all of those things to her, but she'd only see it as interference.

Kicking at a rock, Erik looked up at the sky. Wisps of lacy white clouds were strung out against the brilliant blue. It would rain tomorrow or the next day for sure, and he still had work to do in the fields. Maybe he would give Sigrid another day to think about things and then he would bring up the subject again. *Only this time,* he thought, *I'll find a way to tell her how I feel about her. Surely that would make a difference.*

SMORBAKELSER
(Swedish Butter Cookies)

1 CUP BUTTER	2 CUPS FLOUR
2 EGG YOLKS	1 TSP. ALMOND EXTRACT
½ CUP SUGAR	1 TSP. VANILLA EXTRACT

Oven at 400°F

Cream butter, egg yolks, sugar, and extracts together until light and fluffy. Add flour and mix well. Dough will be soft, but not sticky. Roll out (don't overflour) and cut with cookie cutter or use in cookie press. Bake at 400°F for 8–10 minutes. They burn easily, so be careful.

five

$\mathcal{T}$he September wedding of her widowed friend Ella Swanson gave Sigrid something else to focus on other than work. Ella, with her three fatherless boys, was quite happy to accept an offer of marriage from Per Anderson. The thirty-five-year-old bachelor seemed overly quiet and reserved for Ella's rambunctious bunch, but Sigrid could see that the boys adored the man. And, Ella seemed quite satisfied with the match.

With the weather cooperating perfectly, the wedding supper was held outside in picnic fashion on the church lawn. Sigrid had baked several dishes to bring to the supper, including one of Ella's favorites, smorbakelser, little butter cookies so light and rich that they instantly melt in the mouth. *They appear,* Sigrid thought with a smile, *to be one of Erik's favorites as well.* Seeing him make yet another trip to the dessert table, she watched him grab up a handful of the cookies and plop them down on his plate in a rather possessive manner.

"Oh, there you are," Mrs. Moberg said, coming up from behind Sigrid. "I hoped to talk to you. I heard it said that the railroad is planning to buy your land for a depot. Is that true? What will you do then? Are you going to live with Sven and Olga?"

Taken aback by the rapid interrogation, Sigrid shook her head. "I don't know anything about a depot, and I don't plan to sell the farmstead to the railroad. Where did you get such an idea?"

The robust woman jutted her chin in the air. "Mr. Moberg told me, and where he heard it from, I can't say."

"Well, someone obviously has their facts wrong."

"Wrong about what?" Mrs. Swanson questioned and before waiting for an answer, added, "Don't Ella look nice?"

They all agreed that Ella made a radiant bride before Mrs. Moberg relayed her information on the railroad.

"Ja, I heard there was talk of a depot and round-house for the engines. Your farmstead is a good place for these things."

"That's not my opinion," Sigrid said. "I intend to get down to the bottom of this gossip right away." Leaving the two old women to stare after her in stunned silence, Sigrid went in search of Ruben.

Weaving her way through the crowd, Sigrid felt disheartened at not being able to immediately locate Ruben. She knew he'd been invited to the celebration, and she had counted on seeing him there. It was funny the way he made her feel. Sometimes she welcomed his visits and other times she felt like a creature misplaced in time. He laughed at her crude lifestyle and told her that with the coming of the new century, her way of life would rapidly become obsolete. Still, he made her feel like a woman, all feminine and girlish. She found herself wanting to impress him, and she wanted him to take notice.

Spying him watching a game of horseshoes, Sigrid slipped up from behind and pulled on his coat sleeve. "Can we talk for a moment?"

He flashed her a grin that suggested she'd just made his day, and with a hand to the small of her back, he led her away from the crowd to a nearby stand of trees.

"What would you like to talk about?" he asked, rubbing one of the handlebars of his mustache between his thumb and finger. "I've known weddings to bring even the shyest girl out of her shell."

Sigrid felt her cheeks grow hot. Ruben seemed to imply that she was interested in some kind of romantic tryst, and while she could easily see herself in the role, she had to know the truth about her property.

"I've been told by some of my friends that the

railroad intends to try to build a depot on my land. Maybe even take the entire farmstead for a round-house and such. Is this true, Ruben?" She searched his face, particularly his dark eyes, and waited for some sign that would reassure her.

Ruben took hold of her hand and kissed it lightly. Sigrid found herself trembling from the action and quickly pulled her hand away. "Is it true?" she pressed the question again.

"I have no knowledge of it, if it is," he admitted. "I would have been told if that were the plan, and I know nothing of it."

Sigrid relaxed a bit and sighed. "I hate gossip. It's always getting a person worked up for no reason at all." She felt him move closer to her and thought of moving away. But the notion quickly passed from her mind.

"Sigrid, you are so beautiful. I don't know why you let yourself worry about things. Trust me, I'll find out if there is any truth to the rumors. In the meantime, why don't we spend some time together? We could walk down by the creek and leave the others to their celebration while we have our own private party."

Sigrid stammered at his passionate expression. "I. . .ah. . .I don't think. . ." Before she could finish her words, Ruben pulled her into his arms.

"I don't want you to think about anything but me," he said and kissed her quite soundly on the mouth.

Sigrid stood absolutely rigid as he let her go. She had to remain fixed that way, because she was certain if she so much as took a single step, her knees would buckle from beneath her.

He gently touched the curl of hair that fell over one ear. "You are a magnificent woman, Sigrid. I think I'm losing my heart to you."

Sigrid couldn't look him in the eye. The whole idea of being courted was so foreign to her. For so many years she'd kept her heart completely boxed off, knowing that as the youngest daughter, she was required to care for her mother until the time of her death.

"Don't be afraid to trust your heart," Ruben said

softly. "Come with me."

Sigrid knew it would be impossible to go with him down to the creek. What little reputation she might have managed to keep intact would be ruined for certain if they were to slip away.

"I. . .I need to go," she finally said and turned to walk briskly away.

Ruben did nothing to stop her, and a part of her was hurt by this. If he cared so much about keeping her company, why didn't he at least call after her? But another part of her was just as grateful that he didn't. She'd never been kissed on the mouth before, and it seemed such a glorious and wondrous experience that Sigrid wanted to find a way to go off by herself and contemplate what had just happened.

"I just saw him kiss her," Mrs. Moberg was saying to a collected gathering of older women. "I think that more than suggests what I said was true."

Erik came upon this conversation as he made his fourth trip to the supper tables. His agitation at not being able to spend time alone with Sigrid had made him poor company for everyone else. She was ignoring him, and in the months that had past since his offer to marry her, Sigrid had never allowed him to speak on the matter again. He'd hoped the atmosphere of a wedding might give him the forum to declare his love, but so far Sigrid had remained completely out of his company.

"You know I heard that they were close to an understanding," one of the women continued the conversation.

"Bah!" exclaimed Mrs. Moberg. "I've heard it said that Sigrid has already accepted his proposal. Think on that, our Sigrid married to Ruben Carter. Why I don't imagine she would stay in Lindsborg long after that."

"No, indeed," a third woman countered. "I heard he is rich. Lives in a fancy mansion in Kansas City. No doubt she'd prefer spending the winter in luxury rather than on the prairie."

Erik's chest tightened as the words of the conversation permeated his brain. Sigrid and Carter were engaged? When had this happened?

"Well, from the looks of the way he was kissing her just now, I'd say they'd better do something in a hurry," Mrs. Moberg added in a haughty tone.

Erik left his plate at the table and walked away in a daze. Carter had kissed Sigrid? And she'd let him? Anger slowly welled inside. It seemed to pulsate to life from every part of his body, until there was a hard, black ball knotting up in his stomach. She couldn't be in love with that two-faced, no-good.

"Erik, have you seen my sister?"

Erik glanced up to find Sven coming toward him. "No, but apparently a good many other people have."

Sven stared at him with an expression of confusion. "What do you mean by that?"

Erik started to explain, then bit back the retort and shrugged. "I can't seem to locate her, but I've heard others mention having seen her. She must be around here somewhere."

"Ja, I suppose she's found some way to keep busy."

Erik grimaced. "Yes, I suppose she has."

He walked away quickly, lest he should open his mouth and let pour the anger inside. Hurrying away

65

from the party, Erik found himself taking the long way back to his house. He realized that he wanted nothing more than to find Sigrid and force some sense into her head. And then, he wanted nothing more than to kiss her himself and show her that he meant business.

"I'm powerful angry, Lord," he said, looking skyward. "I don't mean to be, but I am and there's no use denying it. I've tried to be reasonable about things. I've tried to keep my hands and mind busy so that she'd have time to consider my proposal, but it isn't my proposal she's considering."

He slowed his stride as his anger spent itself in prayer. "I don't want to lose her, but how can I convince her that I love her?"

"Just tell her," a voice seemed to say.

Erik stopped in his tracks and glanced around him. Nothing but a few buildings and cornfields greeted his gaze. Maybe God was trying to speak to his heart. Maybe he had relied too long on his own understanding, and now it was time to face doing things another way.

"Have I ignored You, God?" he asked suddenly. Shoving his hands in his pockets, Erik moved on down the lane. He tried to imagine what God would have him do.

"Tell her? But she already knows how I feel about her. After all, I asked her to marry me."

You asked her to marry you so that you could keep her on her land, his heart reminded him. *You said nothing of love.*

"Well, maybe it's time I did," Erik declared, suddenly feeling a bit of his self-confidence return. "After all, they aren't married yet."

EGG GRAVY

2 T. BACON OR SAUSAGE DRIPPINGS	2 T. FLOUR
	2 EGG YOLKS
4 CUPS MILK	½ TSP. SALT

Put meat drippings into a skillet over medium heat. Add flour as you would for gravy. Blend and leave to brown a bit. Mix milk, egg yolks (slightly beaten), and salt, and add to flour and grease. Mix this until thick, but don't allow it to curdle. Add more milk if you like thinner gravy. When mixture is the right consistency for you, remove from heat and serve over Swedish rye bread.

six

*H*arvest was a busy time of year for all of Lindsborg, but Sigrid found it especially trying. It was easy to see now how hard her mother had worked. Even though Tilly was unable to do much of the heavy work, she had prepared the vegetables for canning and helped with the livestock. Now that all of this fell to Sigrid's shoulders, her only saving grace was that the railroad had completed its line and she was no longer needed to feed the workers.

Still, she'd been up by four that morning to do her own chores, and throughout the course of the day, there'd been little opportunity to even pause for the briefest rest. Most of the morning had been spent in cleaning vegetables and the afternoon would be devoted to canning them.

Glancing at the clock, Sigrid was startled to find it was nearly one-thirty, and she hadn't fixed anything for lunch. During harvest time, Erik usually made his way to her house for the noon meal. Since she was already spending most of her time in the kitchen canning, making lunch for the both of them made sense. What didn't make sense was sending Erik back to his own place or even into town for a bite to eat. But now, she'd let it slip her mind completely, and she feared he would show up starving and she'd not have a single morsel prepared.

Staring at the cupboards, trying to decide what would be quickest, Sigrid finally decided egg gravy would be the best solution. Her mother said there was always a meal to be had in egg gravy and rye bread.

Sigrid hoped it would be filling enough to meet with Erik's hearty appetite. She fried up a panful of bacon to go along with it, then used the drippings for the base of her gravy. She had just finished adding the final ingredients when she heard a knock on the back door.

"Come on in, lunch is nearly ready," she called and hurried to slice tomatoes and rye bread.

"Well, I didn't know you were fixing lunch for me," Sven said, lumbering into the kitchen.

"What are you doing here?" she asked in surprise. "I figured you'd be cutting broomcorn."

"Ja, we've been hard to work on it, but something else came up." Her brother's expression appeared a cross between anxious and hesitant.

"So what is it that brings you here?"

"I want to talk to you about our agreement."

"You mean regarding the property?" she asked, turning back to give the gravy a quick stir before removing it from the stove.

"I know I told you that you could have until Christmas, but—" He fell silent as though trying to figure out how best to explain.

"Sven, what are you up to?" she asked flatly. "If it's the money, I can pay you now. I have enough put together to pay both you and Ina. So if that's what you're here for, I can accommodate you."

"No, Sigrid. Sit down."

She sat obediently as a sense of fear ran down her spine. Something had changed his mind. *He's come to break our deal.*

"The railroad has offered to pay double what we talked about," Sven announced. "They are willing to give us three hundred dollars for the farm."

"So they are trying to get this land for a depot and roundhouse. Is that it?" Sigrid asked. Why hadn't Ruben known about this yesterday when she'd asked him?

"I guess that's the idea," Sven replied. "I can't say for sure. Maybe they just want the extra space for a spur line to work on the cars."

"Well, they can't have it!" she declared firmly. "Sven, you've been taught to be a man of honor. Moder would expect you to keep your word, and so do I."

"Be reasonable, Sigrid. That's a hundred dollars a piece. I could use that money and so could Ina, especially now that the new baby is nearly here. She and Clarence barely have room as it is, and a hundred dollars would go a long way to help them build onto the house and get some of the things they need. And, if you're still determined to live alone, a hundred dollars could buy you a little place in town. You wouldn't have to work nearly so hard. You could probably live off that money for a good long time."

"I don't want a place in town, Sven. I want this place. This is my home. Or at least I always thought it was. I love this place. It's a part of Moder and Fader, and I don't want to let that go."

"I'm your brother, and I'm the head of the family now. I'm sorry, Sigrid, but I'm going to talk to Ina about this. I'm sure she'll feel the same way I do." He got to his feet and walked to the back door.

Sigrid had no other choice but to follow after him. "You can't do this. If you love me, you won't do this." She knew the words cut him like a knife.

She could see even with his back turned to her that his shoulders slumped a little lower.

"I'm sorry," was all he could say.

Sigrid's vision blurred with tears. She watched Sven walk away and wished she could think of something to say in order to change his mind. She could never pay him and Ina both one hundred dollars. She barely had enough to pay them the fifty each.

"What did Sven want?" Erik asked, coming from around the corner of the house. His face and arms were still wet from having washed up at the pump.

"To ruin my life," Sigrid barely managed to whisper before fleeing into the house.

She wiped her eyes with the apron, not wanting Erik to see her cry, but he had followed on her heels and knew exactly what was happening.

"What is it? What did he do that would make you cry?"

Sigrid swallowed down a lump in her throat. "He plans to sell the farm to the railroad."

"He can't do that," Erik said, and his expression told Sigrid that he was every bit as upset at the prospect as she was.

"That's what I told him, but he doesn't care. They are offering him three hundred dollars, and I can't possibly match that." She sat down hard on the chair. A thought came to her, but she quickly pushed it aside. If she married Erik, then perhaps they could combine their money and pay Sven and Ina. But no! That was no reason to marry. Besides, the haunting reminder of Ruben's kiss stood between her and Erik now.

"Ruben said he knew nothing about this," she said, mindless of the effect on Erik.

"Apparently he had other things on his mind," Erik said, not even attempting to hide his bitterness.

"What is that supposed to mean?" Sigrid asked.

"There are rumors about you two. I guess you made quite a spectacle of yourself yesterday." He looked at her, seeming to dare her to deny his words.

"It's none of your business," she snapped and got up to bring the food to the table. "You'd better eat before this gets cold."

Erik surprised her by taking hold of her arm and

forcing her to face him. "You can't trust Carter. He isn't one of us. He isn't from around here. He doesn't know the first thing about farming, and you can bet your pretty little head, he doesn't intend to stay in Lindsborg for long."

"Stop it!" Sigrid said, pulling away. "You don't know anything about him. You're just mad because I won't sell you the farm."

"What do you know about how I feel? You haven't bothered to give me so much as two words at one sitting. I come here, you throw food at me, and then I leave to go tend the livestock or garden or go to town. I know you're hurting over this, but you aren't hearing me."

"I've heard enough!"

"Then you don't care that people think you are playing fast and loose with Ruben Carter? You don't care that folks did more talking about you and Carter kissing yesterday than they did discussing Ella's wedding?"

Sigrid felt the heat rise from her collar. She couldn't deny what he was accusing her of, and for reasons she couldn't understand, this only made her angrier. Jerking away, she waved to the food on the counter. "Eat or not, but I refuse to talk to someone who only wants to yell at me!"

She stormed off to her bedroom and slammed the door as loudly as she could to make her point. Turning the key in the lock, she hoped it made enough noise to leave Erik without a doubt as to how she felt about him at that moment.

Throwing herself across the bed, Sigrid began to cry in earnest because she really didn't know how she felt about anything. Especially Erik. Why did this have to be so difficult? She cared a great deal about Erik, but Ruben made her feel so excited and alive. Ruben had only to look at her a certain way, and she trembled from head to foot. Erik certainly never did that for her.

Or had he? She thought back on times when she'd caught him smiling at her a certain way. Her stomach had always seemed to do flip-flops when that happened, but she had always ignored it. *But he doesn't think of me the same way Ruben does,* she thought, and hot tears fell from her eyes. *Ruben desires me as a woman. Erik just thinks of me as a child. He only wants me for the land.*

Beating her hands against the pillow, Sigrid cried until there were no tears left to cry. It was only when she'd dried her eyes and rolled over on her back that she thought to pray.

"Oh, God," she mournfully whispered, "I'm so confused. I don't know what to do. I don't want to leave my home, but it seems that Sven has made up his mind. I have no choice but to do as others direct me to do. But I want You to show me what to do. I want You to guide and direct me. Please help me to know what's right in Your sight, and give me the strength to deal with this matter."

She sighed, feeling only marginally better. There was a kitchen full of work awaiting her attention, and yet all she really wanted to do was sleep. Just sleep and forget the rest of the world and all the problems that went along with it. The coming months would forever see her life changed, and Sigrid wanted to keep things still, if only for a little while.

Giving in to her desires, she closed her eyes and fell asleep. Somehow, God would surely find a way to make it all work out.

POTATISKORV
(Potato Sausage)

6 LARGE RAW POTATOES (PEELED AND GROUND)
1 TSP. PEPPER
2 TSP. SALT
1 TSP. ALLSPICE
1 CUP MILK
1 ½ LBS. GROUND BEEF
2 ½ LBS. GROUND PORK
1 MEDIUM ONION (GROUND)

Mix all ingredients together and stuff into sausage casings, being careful not to overfill as they will expand during cooking. Prick casing several times with a needle before cooking. Put into a pot of hot water and boil over medium heat for 1 hour. Then brown in a frying pan if desired. Makes six 24-inch sausages.

seven

Cold weather set in, and with it came a frenzy to finish up the harvest chores. Sigrid had scarcely seen anything of Erik or Sven since that dreadful day in the kitchen. She felt relieved to have been left to her own concerns, and yet she rather missed seeing Erik at mealtime. With the heavy work of harvest, Sigrid was used to Erik sharing all of her meals, but after that day, he had simply stopped coming.

Her conscience bothered her when she thought about having hurt his feelings. She didn't know where to fit Erik into her life. She knew she had feelings for him, but they certainly weren't the same kind of physical feelings she had for Ruben. On the other hand, she shared very little of common interest with Ruben. They talked on several occasions since he'd stolen the kiss at Ella's wedding, and each time Sigrid tried to imagine herself spending the rest of her life with him.

These thoughts continued to haunt her as she worked to stuff sausage casings with potatiskorv. The potato sausage would be a nice delicacy to have for the holidays, and Sigrid could remember what a favorite it was of her mother's.

"Oh, Moder," she whispered, "I miss you so. Nothing seems right with you gone. I've made such a mess of things."

The sound of the back door opening gave her a start. Had her brother come to torment her with the signing over of her home? Or, had Erik returned to confront her with her behavior?

"Sigrid?"

It was Ruben.

Sigrid was surprised and more than a little bit embarrassed to have Ruben find her in such a state of disarray. Wiping the sausage from her hands, she put a hand up to her hair, hoping desperately that she wouldn't appear too much of a mess.

"I wasn't expecting you," she murmured, trying hard to steady her nerves.

He glanced around and smiled. "I hope I'm not interrupting."

"Only in a pleasant way," she said, beginning to relax. "I've been making sausages all morning and in truth, I could use a rest." She turned back to put a towel over the entire affair and felt a charge of electricity shoot through her when Ruben came to stand directly behind her.

His warm breath on her bare neck caused Sigrid to tremble. Ruben turned her gently and took hold of her shoulders. "I haven't been able to get you out of my mind. I miss coming here on a daily basis." He tilted her face up and studied her for a moment as though inspecting a rare flower. "I can't get this face out of my mind. When I sleep, I dream about you, and when I awaken, I long to see you and to hold you."

Sigrid felt her breath quicken. My, but this man could bring her blood to a boil quicker than anyone she'd ever known.

Ruben took her tenderly into his arms. "I want to kiss you again. May I?"

She was touched that he should ask. "I suppose so."

He lost little time. Lowering his mouth to hers, Ruben pulled her tightly against him. He kissed her with more passion than she'd ever imagined, and it so frightened her that she pulled away panting. Stepping away from him, she stared back, trying to reason inside her what it was that had caused her reaction.

"I'm sorry," he said softly. "I didn't mean to frighten you. It's just that I can no longer fight the feelings I have for you. There's something I want to say and hope you won't think me too forward." His words were methodically delivered, and Sigrid found herself very nearly mesmerized by them.

"What. . .what. . .is it?" she barely managed to croak out.

"I want you to marry me."

She gasped. "What?"

His expression suggested he enjoyed the control he held over her. With a smug grin, he repeated the proposal. "I said that I want you to marry me."

Sigrid couldn't believe that he'd actually just proposed. She felt the warmth of his passionate gaze pierce her facade of indifference. He wanted to marry her!

"Just like that?" she questioned, forcing her wits to resurface.

"Well, of course. I want us to marry right away. We can take a wedding trip to Kansas City and stay in my parents' home. The place is massive and we won't be cramped for room."

"But Lindsborg is my home," she interjected.

"Lindsborg has been your home, but it doesn't have to stay that way."

Sigrid shook her head. "I must say, this comes as a great surprise. We scarcely know each other."

"We know each other better than most folks," he assured her. "Come sit with me and we can talk about all the things that are worrying you." He reached out for her arm, but Sigrid was unsure that she wanted him to touch her. Strange things happened to her mind when he touched her. Seeing her hesitation, Ruben held up his hands and backed away. "Please. Just come sit with me for a time."

Sigrid took a seat and stared at the wall over his head. "All of my family live in Lindsborg. My friends are here. My life is here. I don't want to live in the city. At least I don't think I do."

"But, my dear, you've never seen the city. You've never been outside this tiny town in all of your life. You told me so, remember?" She nodded and he continued. "You have no idea what lies in wait for you out there. The opportunities are too numerous and too wondrous to even imagine. You can never grow bored there."

"I don't grow bored here," she countered.

Looking at Ruben with a new heart, Sigrid tried to honestly see herself in the role of his wife. He dressed immaculately in fine suits and always looked the epitome of style and fashion. His hands were soft and clean, with perfectly trimmed nails and no calluses to mar their appearance. He would no doubt expect just such perfection from a wife.

"Family is very important to me, Ruben. The man I marry will have to understand that, and he will have to honor God, as well. God is the foundation for all I hold true and dear."

"I understand and completely agree with you." The words came without appearance of discomfort.

She got up without warning and walked to the kitchen window. "I've grown to love this house and this land. My parents worked hard to make this a home, and now your railroad wants to destroy all of that and put in their depot and their roundhouse."

"So don't sell it to them."

His words were so matter-of-fact that Sigrid couldn't help but turn to look at him. "Just like that?"

He smiled. "Just like that. Don't sell it and they'll build elsewhere."

"But I thought this location was perfect."

Ruben rubbed his mustache. "It is, and it would make things go a whole lot better for all the people in this town. The railroad doesn't choose a site without weighing heavily the impact it will have on the townspeople. If the people aren't happy, the railroad is doomed to certain failure."

"I hadn't thought about making it easier for everyone else." Suddenly she felt very selfish. "I have to admit, I've only thought of my own pain. My own needs."

Ruben rose to his feet and slowly crossed the room. "As my wife, you need never worry about pain or comfort again. I can give you everything."

"But I have everything I want here."

He smiled tolerantly. "But there's so much more I want to give you. I want to show you the world, and I want to show you to the world. Will you at least think about my proposal?"

Sigrid swallowed hard and nodded. "All right. I'll think about it."

"Good. I'll expect you to give me an answer as soon as possible. After all, the holidays are nearly upon us and I know you'll be far too busy to give much thought over to a wedding then."

Sigrid nodded but said nothing. Her mind was consumed with the weight of Ruben's proposal and all that it might mean to her.

He left without any further attempt to kiss her, even though for a moment Sigrid had feared that had been his definite intent. She turned back to the kitchen counter and sighed. How could she possibly keep her mind on work now?

She finished her tasks just before the last light of day faded into twilight. Lighting the lamps, Sigrid took down her mother's Bible and sat down to read. There had to be answers for the questions in her heart.

Her hand immediately opened to the tenth chapter of Matthew. Scanning down, she came upon verse sixteen, which admonished, "Behold, I send you forth as sheep in the midst of wolves: be ye therefore wise as serpents, and harmless as doves."

Moder had often spoken of Satan's deception in appearing as one of the sheep in order to work his way into the flock.

"If you saw a wolf coming, you would shoot him, ja?" she could hear her mother question. "But when a stray sheep joins in, you think not so very much about it. You figure you will find the owner and return him, but he'll do no harm to graze with your own flock until that time. After all, he's just a sheep."

Erik had warned her that Ruben wasn't all that he appeared—that he wasn't one of them. He told her to mind herself around him, and his brotherly advice bothered her greatly.

Lord, I want to do the right thing. Selling the farm would help Ina and Sven in ways that I can't hope to help them. Giving this land up would benefit the town, and all of my friends and family would have a better life because of my sacrifice. She closed the Bible and laid her head atop it. *I don't mean to put a thing or place above the comfort and need of my loved ones. I guess I'm ready to let go, if that's what You want me to do. It doesn't feel good or right, but if You want me to do this thing, then please mark out the path.*

And as for Ruben and his proposal. She paused, trying to figure out what she should pray. *You know what he's asked of me, and You alone know if he's the one for me. I just feel so confused. There's Ruben, and then there's Erik. Ruben has asked me to marry him, and he seems to genuinely love me. Erik has asked me to marry him, and he seems to genuinely care about me, but I'm not so sure he loves me.*

And whom do you love? her heart seemed to ask.

"I wish I knew," she answered aloud.

Jast Krans
Yeast Wreath

1 PACKAGE YEAST	4 CUPS FLOUR
3 T. SUGAR	1 TSP. SALT
3 EGG YOLKS	1 CUP BUTTER
1 CUP WARM MILK	

Dissolve together yeast, sugar, and ½ cup warm milk; set aside. Next, beat together egg yolks and ½ cup warm milk; set aside. Mix together flour, salt, and butter (this will be like pie crust). Add the yeast and egg yolk mixtures and mix well. Set in a cool place overnight.

3 EGG WHITES	1 TSP. CINNAMON
½ CUP SUGAR	HANDFUL OF NUTS,
	DATES, OR RAISINS (IF DESIRED)

Oven at 350°F

In the morning, divide dough into two portions and roll out thin. Mix 3 stiffly beaten egg whites with sugar and cinnamon and spread this on top of the dough. Sprinkle with nuts, dates, or raisins. Roll lengthwise and shape in a ring. Let rise 1 hour or until doubled. Bake at 350°F for 20 minutes. Frost with ¾ cup powdered sugar blended with cream.

eight

*E*rik sat in the cafe nursing his third cup of coffee. For longer than he cared to remember, he'd been coming here for meals instead of going to the Larsson house. He felt it was only fair to give Sigrid her head. She was going to have to decide for herself if he meant anything to her—anything more than friends and workers of the same ground.

Putting the cup down, Erik decided it was time

to return to the fields. But just as he reached for his hat, the unmistakable voice of Ruben Carter sounded from the now open cafe door.

"Come on, Hank, I'll treat you to lunch and tell you where things stand."

Erik froze in place, wondering if he should confront Carter with his concern for Sigrid. He wanted badly to warn the man to leave her alone, but it wasn't his place and so he held himself in check.

Carter, clearly oblivious to anyone else in the cafe, took the booth directly behind Erik and continued his conversation. Never one to set out to eavesdrop, Erik couldn't help himself when Carter brought up the subject of Sigrid and the farmstead.

"I figure if I can get her to marry me before Christmas," Carter told his companion, "I can get her to sign over without too much difficulty."

"You mean you'll keep her so otherwise occupied she won't have time to worry about land, don't ya?" the man said with a dirty laugh.

Carter chuckled. "Well, that will be one of the benefits of this whole scheme. She's not that bad to look at, although she's the same as the rest of these dirt-dumb farmers. She's actually happy to live here and wants to stay in Lindsborg."

"Maybe that'll change after you propose."

"I proposed yesterday," Carter admitted.

Erik hadn't realized how hard he was gripping the coffee mug until his hand started to ache. He put the cup down and tried to refrain from jumping to his feet. He couldn't confront Carter here. Not this way. Not now.

"Did she say yes?" the other man was now questioning.

"Not exactly, but I did my best to persuade her, if you know what I mean."

They laughed in a way that left Erik little doubt that Carter had probably handled the matter in a most inappropriate way. But, he knew Sigrid, and he felt confident that she had probably put Carter in his place in spite of what the man said to his friend.

"Sigrid will come around, and when she does," Carter continued, "the land will be ours."

"I thought you had a deal with that brother of hers. Seems a sorry state of affairs that you should have to hitch yourself up with her in order to get the land."

"Her brother's willing to sell me the place, but he hates hurting Sigrid. I tried to play it smooth, let him think I understood his compassion. I let it drop and figured I'd work on Sigrid. If I can talk her into marriage, I shouldn't have any trouble getting her to give up the farm. After all, I made it clear that Kansas City could offer us both a great deal in the way of comfort and charm. After a couple of months there, I'll send her home to her brother. Then she can have her farm town and the railroad can have their depot and roundhouse."

"You mean divorce her?"

"Of course. I don't intend to stay married to someone like her," Carter said in a voice that suggested how unthinkable such a matter could be. "Imagine trying to take her to New York. She could never hope to fit into my social circle. No, I've spent enough time listening to her stories of Swedish traditions and love of the land. I'll be glad to knock the dust of this town off my feet once and for all."

"But you'll have a good time with her first, I hope," the man said in a much lowered voice.

Carter laughed. "Of course. I don't mind sampling country cooking. I just don't want it for the rest of my life."

The men laughed while Erik seethed. He wanted to punch Carter square in the nose, but more than that, he wanted to run to Sigrid and hide her away like a precious gem. How dare Carter talk of using her and then divorcing her! How would Sigrid ever live with the shame of such a thing?

The waitress came to serve the two men, and with her keeping them both completely occupied, Erik slipped out the back door of the cafe. He struggled to know what he should do. On one hand, if he went to Sigrid and told her the truth, she might not believe him. She might think that he was only speaking out of a jealous heart or, worse yet, that he only wanted to keep her from giving Carter the land.

"Lord," he whispered, stepping into the dusty

alley, "this isn't an easy situation to be in. I don't know what to do to protect Sigrid." He paused and glanced heavenward with a smile. "But then again, I don't need to protect her when You're already on the job."

He walked down the alley and around the building, continuing to pray. *She needs to be kept safe, Lord. I don't know if I should tell her what I overheard or leave it be. You know the answers, and You have a better picture of the truth than I do. What should I do?*

Erik paused beside the general store and looked down Main Street at their little town. He loved it here, and he knew Sigrid loved it as well. The land and the community were as much a part of him as anything could possibly be, and he couldn't imagine his life in any way that didn't include living in Lindsborg.

Feeling his turmoil only moderately relieved, Erik sighed and made his decision. *If she asks me straight forward for the truth, I'll tell her. Otherwise, I won't volunteer anything.*

Moving down the street, another even more compelling thought came to mind. *What I need to do is ensure that she doesn't marry Ruben Carter.* He smiled to himself. *I just need to convince her that she should marry me instead of him.* Then his smile faded. Never having been one for romancing and courting women, especially given the fact that his eye had been on Sigrid for more than a decade, Erik wondered exactly how he should go about it.

As if on cue, Sigrid appeared—basket in hand—heading toward the general store. Erik swallowed hard. She looked wonderful. Her cheeks were rosy from the chill in the air, and her eyes were bright and searching. He stepped out of the shadows and smiled, hoping she would smile in return—praying she wouldn't give him a cold shoulder.

"Erik!" she exclaimed, seeming surprised but genuinely happy to see him. "I haven't seen you in forever."

The ease with which she spoke put Erik's pounding heart at rest. "I went to help Sven with the broomcorn."

"Oh," she said, nodding as if understanding some great mystery. "Have you finished?"

"Yes."

The silence hung between them for several moments. "Have you come to town for something in particular?" Erik finally asked.

"Oh, you know, the usual holiday things. With Advent, St. Lucia's Day, and all that goes with Christmas, I don't dare run out of sugar and flour. Not with all of my nieces and nephews to bake for. Oh, and I need some almonds. At least one almond," she said as if trying to burn it into memory.

Erik smiled. "Ah, making Risgrynsgrot?" He spoke of the favorite rice pudding that was always found at any Swedish Christmas celebration. The trick was to mix in one whole almond and whoever found it in their portion of pudding was said to be the next one to marry or have good fortune.

"Yes, that and about a hundred other things." She smiled and her blue eyes lit up as an idea appeared to come to her. "Say, if you aren't busy, why don't you come for dinner tonight? I'm trying out a new recipe for jast krans, and I'd love for you to tell me what you think of it."

Erik felt his breathing quicken. It was as if their last meeting had never happened. She beamed her smile and talked as friendly and openly as she'd ever talked to him before. She was beautiful and charming and everything he longed for. Why couldn't she see that his love for her was sincere? "I'd like to come for dinner," he finally answered in a low, steady voice.

"Good. I'll see you at the usual time then." She turned to go into the general store, but Erik reached out to touch her arm.

"I. . .uh. . ."

"Yes?" She looked up at him, her eyes widening.

Erik felt unsure of himself. "It's just that, well. . ." What could he say? What should he say—that he missed her? That a moment didn't pass by during the day that he wasn't thinking of her? "Thanks for the invitation."

She nodded, and for a moment Erik almost thought he read disappointment in her eyes. Had she expected him to say something more?

He let her go and stared at the door to the general store for several minutes before ambling down the street. *Where do I go from here?* he wondered. He wondered, too, at her good mood and her pleasantries. Then a thought came unbidden to his mind. Maybe Carter's proposal had brought this about. Maybe her joy centered around contemplating a lifetime as the wife to Ruben Carter.

Erik frowned and his optimism faded. Maybe her invitation for dinner had been given in order to break the news to him. What if she announced that she planned to accept Carter's proposal? Erik felt his stomach tighten and begin to churn. There had to be some way to convince her that he loved her.

Tell her that you love her, his heart told him. *Sit her down and tell her the truth?* It was almost too much to think about, and Erik did the only thing that felt right and comfortable. He found his horse and went back to work.

Later that night, after a quiet dinner with Sigrid,

Erik found himself no closer to revealing the truth of his heart to Sigrid. She had presented him with a wonderful meal, but had gone to no special lengths to entertain him. She talked of her sister Ina and the baby that was on the way. She asked him if he would keep an eye on the house for her as she planned to spend the next few weeks with her sister.

"With the baby due," she had told Erik, "Ina isn't up to the usual holiday cooking. I promised I'd come lend a hand, and since she is on the other side of town, I thought I'd just as well stay on at her place."

Before he knew it, Erik had agreed to care for her livestock and watch over the house, but he hadn't found the right opportunity in which to share his heart. Kneeling beside his bed in prayer, Erik found a restlessness inside that would not be ignored.

"Father, help me," he murmured. "Help me to win her heart."

LUSSEKATTER
St. Lucia Buns

2 PACKAGES ACTIVE DRY YEAST	½ CUP DARK RAISINS (OPTIONAL)
¾ CUP SUGAR	1 CUP MILK (SCALDED)
½ CUP SOFTENED BUTTER	6 CUPS FLOUR
1 TSP. SALT	2 EGGS
½ TSP. POWDERED SAFFRON (DISSOLVED IN 2 TSP. OF MILK)	1 TSP. GROUND CARDAMOM
	½ CUP BLANCHED ALMONDS (GROUND)
	¾ CUP LUKEWARM WATER

Oven at 350°F

Soften yeast in lukewarm water. Dissolve thoroughly and add milk and sugar. Beat in 2 cups of the flour until mixture is smooth. Add butter, eggs, salt, raisins, almonds, cardamom, and saffron. Mix well. Add remaining flour and knead until dough is smooth and elastic.

Place dough in greased bowl, cover, and let rise approximately 1½ hours. Punch down and let rise again for 30–40 minutes. Shape into various Lucia bun forms (description contained in chapter) and let rise for another 15–20 minutes. Bake at 350°F for 10–12 minutes. Makes 30–40 buns.

n i n e

*I*t was already December 12, and with the celebration honoring St. Lucia being tomorrow, Sigrid would need to hurry to have the St. Lucia buns ready for the holiday. Pulling the dough from where it had risen, Sigrid began to form the buns into a variety of shapes.

First she made the priest locks or judge's wigs, as some called them. These were long thin strips, rolled in hand and shaped on top of each other until it resembled the old powdered wigs that magistrates wore in court. Each strip was curled up at the end to touch the curl above it. Next, Sigrid formed Christian crosses and Bethlehem stars. Then, just to keep with Swedish tradition, she made a great many buns in the shape of the Julbock, the Christmas goat. Legend claimed that the goat would bring Christmas toys to good Swedish children. Straw replicas of the Julbock could be found in most of the Lindsborg homes during the Christmas season, and the children expected to find them on the Lucia platter.

The knock at Ina's kitchen door startled Sigrid for only a moment. Clarence was gone to town with the children in hopes of purchasing a Christmas gift for Ina. And, since Ina was sleeping, Sigrid had no other choice but to answer the door herself.

There stood Erik, with a light dusting of snow on his shoulders and head, his cheeks reddened from the wind and cold.

"What are you doing here?" she asked, mindless of her manners.

Erik laughed. "I came to see you."

"Well, you'd best come in then," she said, not understanding why she felt awkward in his presence.

Sigrid went back to the oven and checked on the buns. "Have a seat and I'll get you some coffee." Her heart skipped a beat, and her stomach felt like a swirl of butterflies resided inside.

If it's possible, she thought, *he's more handsome than ever.* Then she pushed aside that line of thinking and tried to steady her nerves. Ever since she'd had him to supper the week before, he'd acted all tongue-tied and strange. She'd wondered what he was thinking, but it seemed rude to press him for an answer.

"Smells mighty good in here," Erik said.

Sigrid straightened and went to the cupboard for a cup. "I'm baking the St. Lucia buns," she told him and poured steaming coffee into the mug. "Ina's not feeling very good. I'm guessing the baby will probably come tonight or tomorrow."

She put the coffee down on the table before realizing that Erik held a wrapped package in his hands.

"This is for you," he said, holding out the gift.

"For me?" She knew her voice registered distress

and disbelief. "It's too early for Jul gifts."

"It's not for Jul," he said quite seriously. "I've been doing a lot of thinking, and there're some things that need settled between us."

She felt her mouth go down. "There are?"

"Just open the package and I'll explain."

She sat down at the table and pulled at the strings that held the paper in place. The paper fell away and inside she found two artfully carved wooden spoons. Tears came to her eyes.

"You know what these spoons represent," he more stated than questioned. She nodded but said nothing. "I figured it was time to speak my mind, Sigrid. I don't want to lose you to that Carter fellow. He's boasting all over town how he asked you to marry him, and I'm not giving you up without a fight."

Her head snapped up at this. "You want the land that bad?"

Erik slammed his fists down on the table. "It has nothing to do with the land. I want to marry you. I know how you hold to tradition, so I carved the spoons for you and I'm here to ask you to be my wife."

Still she said nothing. She couldn't speak. Between the tears that were overrunning her eyes and the lump in her throat, Sigrid was afraid to even try to talk.

"I know you think this is about the land, but it isn't," he continued. "Seeing that I have competition and that there's a real possibility you might slip away gave me cause to think. I don't want to lose you, Sigrid. I've loved you since you were a little girl."

At this Sigrid couldn't sit and face him any longer. All she'd ever hoped for was that he might actually declare his love for her. Why did he have to wait until now? Now, when Ruben was offering her the world. She walked away from the table, clutching the spoons to her breast. *What do I do?*

"Did you hear me, Sigrid? I love you. I want you to marry me." Erik came to where she stood with her back to him. He gently put his hands on her arms as if to turn her to face him.

This only caused Sigrid to draw her shoulders in tighter. She couldn't face him. She'd been such a fool. Tears streamed down her cheeks. *He loves me. He wants to marry me because he loves me.* The wonder of it all was too much.

With a low groan that seemed something between anguish and anger, Erik dropped his hold and walked away. Sigrid thought he was taking his seat at the table until she heard the door open and close. She wanted to run after him and had actually turned to get her coat when Ina called to her. Erik would have to wait.

Throughout the night, Ina suffered in heavy labor to give birth to her sixth child. Sigrid stayed by her side, wiping her brow and praying. The breech-positioned infant girl was finally delivered by the doctor just after midnight, and Ina immediately bestowed the name of Bothilda upon the child. It was understood that she would be called Tilly, and Clarence thought it extremely good fortune that she had been born on St. Lucia's Day.

Sigrid's head had barely hit the pillow when Bridgett, the eldest daughter of the family, donned her white robe with the red sash. Yawning, Sigrid forced herself to get out of bed.

"I'll help you with the crown," she said, stifling a yawn.

Bridgett, taking her role as the Lucia Bride or Queen of Lights very seriously, nodded and positioned the wreath on her head and gingerly made her way down the loft stairs. Sigrid followed, finishing up the buttons of her dress as she went.

Bridgett arranged buns and cups on a tray while Sigrid made coffee.

"I love this day," Bridgett announced. "I always feel so special."

"I envy you," Sigrid said, yawning once again. "I never got to be the Lucia Bride when I was growing up. In fact, as youngest, I didn't have a lot of privileges."

"Moder says you made a wonderful sacrifice to insure the happiness and well-being of your family."

Sigrid couldn't hide her surprise. "Ina said that?"

"Sure." Bridgett brought out the candles and handed them to Sigrid. "She said you did her a special favor by taking care of Mormor. She was afraid that since she'd just married Fader, she might have to take Mormor to live with them, and," Bridgett giggled for the first time that day, "she wanted to have Fader all to herself."

Sigrid smiled. "I can well imagine." She positioned the candles, thinking of Ina's gratitude and how she'd not only felt those things but shared them with her daughter as well. It was rather like an honor, and Sigrid suddenly loved Ina more than ever.

Bridgett waited while Sigrid lit the last of the candles. She held the platter proudly and smiled. "Well, here I go." She took a deep breath and began to sing. "Sankta Lucia, ljusklara hagring, Sprid i var vinter natt, glans av den fagring."

Sigrid smiled and thought of the words. "Santa Lucia, thy light is glowing, Through darkest winter night, comfort bestowing." She thought of their traditions and how they honored this young martyr. Legend in Sweden held that Lucia, a young medieval saint, brought food to the hungry in southern Sweden. But Sigrid also knew the celebration to date back even further. The first Lucia was a young Christian girl who gave her entire bridal dowry away to the poor folk of her village. She was later accused of witchcraft and burned at the stake on December 13, in the year 304 A.D. But no matter which Lucia one considered, Sigrid knew that the celebration was a representation of sending light into the darkness.

"Lucia brings the symbol of the light to come," her moder had told her when she was very young. "Jesus is the light who comes to us and makes our darkest night to shine as day."

Sigrid wrapped her arms around her. She could hear Bridgett singing to her family, and the sound left an aching in her heart. She had no family to celebrate with. As the spinster aunt, she had to borrow upon her sibling's family. A tear slid down her cheek and the only thing she desired in that moment was to find Erik and tell him that she loved him.

"I love him," she whispered. "How could I have ever doubted it?"

Suddenly, even the thought of kissing Ruben sounded less than appealing. How had she managed to get so completely swept away? Was she so desperate for affection and attention that she couldn't see how Erik's quiet love had been there all along?

Kottbullar
Swedish Meat Balls

½ LB. GROUND BEEF
2 EGGS (BEATEN)
½ CUP CREAM
   (HEATED TO A BOIL)
¼ TSP. ALLSPICE

½ LB. GROUND PORK
½ CUP BREAD CRUMBS
½ TSP. SALT
⅓ TSP. PEPPER
3 T. ONION
   (FINELY MINCED)

Oven at 325°F

Soak bread crumbs in cream and set aside. Blend the remaining ingredients together. Pour cream and softened bread crumbs into meat mixture and mix well. Roll into balls the size of walnuts and fry until outside is browned. Put into a baking dish with 2 T. oil and 1 T. water, cover and bake at 325°F for 1 hour.

t e n

Sigrid barely waited until the sun was fully risen before pulling on her coat and boots. With mysterious excuses delivered to Ina and Clarence, she made her way home in the pale pink light of dawn. Grateful that there was only a faint dusting of snow on the ground, Sigrid pressed toward town with only one thought in mind. . .Erik.

She had to find him. She had to tell him how

she felt and how she'd ignored those feelings for most of her life. He'd always just been there: comforting, familiar, loving, although she couldn't see it for the nearness of it. Feeling a song in her heart, she hummed Santa Lucia and forced herself not to run.

Chilled to the bone, but warm in spirit, Sigrid crossed Lindsborg's Main Street and hurried in the direction of home. She'd just passed from town when Ruben came from seemingly nowhere.

"Sigrid! I was hoping to see you today. I was just on my way to your house."

She stopped and looked at him sternly, wondering what it was about him that had held her captive for so long.

"What?" Ruben questioned. "Isn't my hat on straight?" He reached up as if to adjust it.

"No, it isn't that," she smiled, not realizing how appealing she looked.

Ruben swept her into his arms, mindless of the very public scene they were making. "I've come for an answer to my proposal. You've put me off long enough." He tried to kiss her, but Sigrid turned her face away and pushed at his arms.

"Let me go, Ruben. I can't marry you."

Ruben dropped his hold and stared at her in surprise. "What do you mean, you can't marry me?"

"I don't love you, Ruben. I can't marry you because I'm in love with someone else. I'm sorry." She didn't wait for his response but instead kept walking toward home. Home and Erik. She knew he'd be close by, and whether he was caring for her livestock or working in his own barn, she would find him and declare her love to him.

"You can't be serious," Rueben said, catching up to her.

She picked up speed and nodded. "But I am."

He grabbed her and pulled her away from the road. Pushing her up against the thick trunk of a cottonwood tree, he glared at her. "You can't do this to me. I have plans."

"I'm sorry." His grip tightened. "Let me go, Ruben."

"No. You're being stupid. It isn't like something better is going to come along."

She smiled. "Something better already has come along. I just didn't realize that he'd been there all along."

"You're coming with me. We're getting married."

Sigrid's mouth dropped open as Ruben dragged her along behind him. She began protesting, yelling, almost screaming for him to leave her alone. Then suddenly, without warning, Sigrid felt her free arm being pulled in the opposite direction. Looking back, she found Erik.

"Let her go, Carter. You heard for yourself, she wants nothing to do with you."

Ruben dropped his hold, completely intimidated by the huge Swede. He opened his mouth as if to say something, then growled and took off in the direction of Main Street.

Sigrid looked up at Erik, not knowing what to say. Her heart was full to bursting with the love she felt inside. He had come to save her once again.

Erik said nothing, but simply took hold of her arm and led her home.

Once inside the warmth of her kitchen, Sigrid felt shy and uncertain. What if she declared her love and Erik no longer wanted her? She swallowed her pride and decided the best thing to do was be honest.

"I didn't expect to see you today," Erik said softly.

"I know." She tried to think of what to say next. "I had to see you."

"Why?"

She drew a deep breath and faltered. Lowering her gaze, she looked at her hands.

"Why, Sigrid?" Erik repeated.

"Because I love you," she whispered.

"What?"

She looked up and found him smiling. He'd heard all right, but he wanted to hear the words again. "I came home to tell you that I love you, and if you still think you want to marry me, then I'd love nothing more."

Erik laughed. "I suppose I could tolerate the idea."

Sigrid smiled and raised a single brow. "Only tolerate?"

"Well, I guess you've got me there."

He got to his feet and came to take her in his arms. Sigrid melted against him, feeling her heart pounding so hard that she was certain he could hear it. She looked up into his eyes and found all the love she'd hoped to find. "Do I really have you?" she whispered.

Just before his lips touched her in a passionate kiss, Sigrid heard him whisper, "You've always had me."

After the Julotta services at church on Christmas morning, Erik and Sigrid joined the rest of her family at Ina's house. The smorgasbord was laid out with all of the traditional foods of their ancestry. Pickled herring, Swedish meat balls, lutefisk, ostkaka, and of course, rice pudding were among the many overflowing platters of goodies.

Sven offered a prayer at Ina's request, and as he finished, Erik requested everyone's attention to announce that he and Sigrid were to be married as soon as the holidays were completed.

"Oh, Sigrid!" Ina squealed in girlish delight. "I'm so happy for you."

Sigrid embraced her sister. "That's not all. Erik and I intend to pay you and Sven the same amount of money that the railroad is offering for the farm. We want to live on the farmstead. I want to raise our children where Moder and Fader worked so hard to make us happy."

Erik lost no time in pulling papers from his pocket. "I know it's Christmas, but this is to show you we mean what we say." He handed the papers to Sven. "I hope you will understand how much this means to both of us."

"Of course we understand," Ina said.

"But I struck an agreement with the railroad," Sven replied rather sheepishly.

"No money changed hands," Ina reminded him. "Besides, I never agreed to it. Erik talked to me some time ago, and I thought his proposal was much better."

Just then a knock sounded on the door and

Bridgett went to open it. Ruben Carter didn't wait to be announced but pushed his way past the girl and came to where Sven was still studying the paper Erik had given him.

"I want to finish our agreement," he told Sven.

"Sorry you had to come all this way, Mr. Carter," Ina said before Sven could reply. "We aren't selling the land to the railroad. Sven had no right to make an agreement without Sigrid's and my approval."

"He's the man of the family, isn't he?" He glared at Sigrid as he asked the question.

"Ja," Ina replied, "but Swedish women are just as tenacious as Swedish men."

"Sorry, Mr. Carter," Sven offered apologetically. "I guess I'm outvoted."

"But we had an agreement."

"It wasn't a lawful arrangement, Carter," Erik said, moving in between Ruben and Sven. "But this is." He took the papers from Sven and held them up. "I'm buying the property with my wife."

Ruben threw Sigrid a sneering look of disbelief. "He's only doing this to get your land."

Sigrid didn't want to face him in an argument. "No, he did it because he loves me," she said as she turned and walked from the room to avoid any further confrontation.

Taking herself outside, Sigrid prayed that the matter would be concluded without her. She didn't like the way Ruben looked at her, and she didn't want to listen to his threats or foul-mouthed accusations. Walking the full length of the wraparound porch, Sigrid had just come to the front when an angry Ruben bounded out of the house. He instantly saw her and stopped.

"I never wanted you for my wife. I wanted the land, just like Lindquist." The words were delivered with all the hate and bitterness that Ruben's face featured. "You aren't worth the trouble, Sigrid." He stormed down the path and left her to stare after him.

His words should hurt, she thought. But they didn't. She only felt sorry for Ruben and more sure of Erik. What did hurt was that she had ever believed Ruben's flowery words of love.

Turning away, she found Erik standing at the end of the porch. He'd heard everything Ruben had said, and he seemed to watch her for any sign of regret in her choice. And then, Sigrid saw something more in his expression. He showed no surprise or alarm at the words he'd heard. Only patient compassion as he waited for her reaction. *He knew! He knew all along and yet he never told me!* Her heart swelled with love for him, and she smiled.

Erik held open his arms and Sigrid eagerly went to him, cherishing the warmth he provided against the cold of winter and Ruben's declaration.

"You knew, did you?" she whispered as he kissed the top of her head.

"Yes."

"And you never told me because you knew I wouldn't have believed you."

"Yes." He kissed her again.

"I was such a fool, Erik."

"Yes." This time he lifted her chin with his warm, callused fingers and kissed her on the forehead.

"Moder always said I could trust you. I should

have believed her. . .and you."

"Yes." He kissed her right cheek.

"I guess love was so close I just couldn't see it. Forgive me?"

"Yes." His low, husky voice warmed her as much as the kiss he placed on her left cheek.

Sigrid smiled and pressed herself closer. "Love me?"

"Oh, yes," he half moaned, half whispered, and pressed his lips to hers.

Sigrid sighed and wrapped her arms around his neck. She returned his kiss with matched enthusiasm and felt the heat of passion radiate throughout her body.

He pulled away, and Sigrid opened her eyes to find him grinning as though he'd just won first place in a race. "God Jul, Darling," he whispered.

"Merry Christmas to you." She strained on tiptoe and pulled his face back to hers. "The first of many." She kissed him gently.

"Kisses or Christmases?" he whispered as their lips parted.

"What?"

"The first of many kisses or Christmases?" he teased.

She didn't hesitate. Kissing him again, she pulled away to whisper in his ear, "Both."